SOOTFACE

A Doubleday Book for Young Readers

SOOTFACE

An Ojibwa Cinderella Story

Retold by Robert D. San Souci

Illustrated by Daniel San Souci

NOTE: This well-known story seems to be primarily a tale of the Northeast and Great Lakes tribes, such as the Ojibwa and other Algonquian (Algonkian) groups, Canada's Micmac people, and so on. I have also come across a variant from a Pueblo storyteller in the Southwest, indicating that this popular tale has traveled widely among Native Peoples.

Among the more than two dozen versions I consulted, some of the most helpful were "Invisible One" in C. G. Leland's *Algonquin Legends of New England* (Boston: Houghton Mifflin Co., 1884), "Oochigeaskw, the Little Scarred Girl" in E. N. Partridge's *Glooscap the Great Chief and Other Stories of the Micmacs* (New York: Macmillan Co., 1913), and "The Algonquin Cinderella" in Indries Shah's *World Tales* (New York: Harcourt Brace Jovanovich, 1979).

The illustrations are based on extensive research at the Anthropology Library of the University of California at Berkeley. Details of clothing, traditional design, and setting reflect mid-eighteenth-century Ojibwa village life.

A Doubleday Book for Young Readers Published by Delacorte Press
Bantam Doubleday Dell Publishing Group, Inc. / 1540 Broadway / New York, New York 10036
Doubleday and the portrayal of an anchor with a dolphin are trademarks of
Bantam Doubleday Dell Publishing Group, Inc.
Text copyright © 1994 by Robert D. San Souci
Illustrations copyright © 1994 by Daniel San Souci

Library of Congress Cataloging in Publication Data
San Souci, Robert D.
Sootface : an Ojibwa Cinderella story / retold by Robert D. San Souci ; illustrated by Daniel San Souci.
p. cm.
Summary: Although she is mocked and mistreated by her two older sisters, an Indian maiden wins a mighty invisible warrior for her husband with her kind and honest heart.
ISBN 0-385-31202-4
1. Ojibwa Indians—Legends.   [1. Ojibwa Indians—Legends.   2. Indians of North America—Legends.]
I. San Souci, Daniel, Ill.   II. Title   E99.C6S32   1994   398.2'089'973—dc20   [E]   93-10553   CIP   AC

Typography by Lynn Braswell
Manufactured in Italy
June 1994
10   9   8   7   6   5   4   3   2

For Allen Say, in friendship and admiration
D.S.S.

For Frances Graves, with warmest thanks
for her friendship, support, and
unfailing good humor
R.S.S.

Once, an Ojibwa man whose wife had died raised three daughters alone. They lived in a village beside a lake, deep in a forest of birch.

The sisters were supposed to share the work of gathering firewood, cooking food, and sewing clothes from skins their father provided.

The two older girls, though pretty enough, were lazy and bad-tempered. When their father was away hunting, they gave most of the work to their youngest sister. The flames from the cooking fire singed her hair and burned her skin. Sometimes her sisters beat her and smeared her face with ashes. Then they made fun of her and called her Sootface.

Poor Sootface's eyes were always sad and tired, but her sisters only gave her more work. At evening her eldest sister cried, "Hurry, lazy Sootface! Fetch some wood to make a fire. Cook the deer meat, for we are hungry."

In the morning, her middle sister said, "Hurry, lazy Sootface! Clean the ashes from last night's fire. Brush the mats, gather berries, and bring fresh water. Our father will soon return from hunting."

When the hunter returned, he saw poor Sootface and asked, "What has happened to my youngest child?"

The eldest sister said, "That one is so clumsy, she fell over her own feet and rolled through the ashes."

And the middle sister said, "We tell her to be careful, not to go too near the fire, but she will not heed us."

Sootface was too afraid of her sisters to argue; she just kept on working. All the while, she sang a little song to herself:

> *Oh, I am thinking,*
> *Oh, I am dreaming,*
> *That even ugly as I am,*
> *I will someday find a husband.*

Her sisters took the best skins to make dresses and moccasins for themselves. Sootface had only scraps to sew into a skirt and a worn-out pair of her father's moccasins, grown stiff with age. When she walked to the lake to fetch water, the young men would nudge each other and point and laugh.

Now, there was a mighty warrior who lived with his sister in a wigwam across the lake from the village. A great medicine man had given him the power to make himself invisible. No one from the village had ever seen him, though they saw his white moccasins when his sister hung them beside the door flap. They saw the flap rise and fall when he entered or left his wigwam.

The villagers knew he was a great hunter, for they watched his sister skin and dry all the deer, elk, and other game that her brother brought her. Though no one but his sister could see him, the women of the village were sure that he was very handsome.

One day, the invisible warrior told his sister, "Go to the village across the water, and say that I will marry the woman who can see me. This means that she has a kind and honest heart. Each day I will carry my magic bow. The woman who tells you what my bow and bowstring are made of will be my bride."

His sister brought this message to the village people. One by one the young women came to visit the lone wigwam. Each carefully braided her hair, dressed in her softest deerskin skirt and moccasins, and wore her finest necklaces of shells or beads.

The invisible hunter's sister greeted each young woman kindly. But when she asked them to tell her what her brother looked like, and what his bow and bowstring were made of, each young woman failed the test, and was sent home.

This went on for a long time. At last, Sootface's eldest sister said that she was going to visit the invisible hunter.

She brushed her hair until it gleamed, and had Sootface braid it for her. Then she went on her way, wrapped in her best deerskin robe and wearing her finest beaded moccasins. She met the hunter's sister beside the lake. Soon they saw white moccasins approaching.

"Can you see my brother?" asked his sister.

"Oh, yes," lied the eldest sister.

"Of what is his bow made?"

"Birch."

"And with what is it strung?"

"Rawhide."

"You did not see my brother," the other woman said.

The eldest sister went home in a bad temper. She yelled at Sootface and gave her more work to do.

The middle sister, who thought herself clever, decided to try her luck. She hung strings of pale shells at her throat and had Sootface weave some into her long braids. Off she went, sure she would become the lucky bride.

As she walked with the hunter's sister, she saw the white moccasins approaching. Quickly, she said, "Here comes your brother now."

"Of what is his bow made?" asked the hunter's sister.

"Horn," said the middle sister, thinking of the finest bow she could imagine.

"And with what is it strung?"

"Braided horsehair," said the middle sister, pleased at her own cleverness.

But the other woman shook her head. "You have not seen my brother."

The middle sister arrived home in a fury. She scolded Sootface and smeared more ashes on her face.

The next day, Sootface decided to visit the hunter's lodge as her sisters had done. She begged her eldest sister, "Sister, let me wear your white shell necklace, softest skirt, and moccasins. I want to go and seek a husband."

But her sister refused, saying, "You would only make my clothes as sooty as yourself."

Then Sootface begged her second sister, "Sister, help me wash and braid my hair, so I may go and seek a husband."

But her sister said, "The fire has burned your hair too short to braid. And I do not want my hands dirtied by the ash that clings to you."

Sootface was stung by their unkindness. But she was determined to present herself to the warrior and his sister. She went alone into the woods. There she said, "Sister birch tree, share your soft white skin with me. Then I can wear a new skirt when I go to seek a husband."

Sootface took strips of birch bark and sewed them together to make a skirt. She wove herself a necklace of wildflowers, and soaked her old, stiff moccasins in a spring until they grew softer. Next, she washed her face and hair as best she could. Her hair was too short to braid, so she added flowers to it, all the while singing:

> *Soon, I am thinking,*
> *Soon, I am dreaming,*
> *That I will find a husband.*
> *I am sure it will be so.*

But when she passed through the village, dressed in the finery the forest had provided, her eldest sister cried, "You are so ugly and foolish-looking, go inside at once!"

"You will shame us before the hunter and his sister," called Sootface's middle sister.

But Sootface walked on as though they were no more than chattering birds in the trees.

When her sisters saw that she would not listen to them, they began to laugh at her. To friends and neighbors, the eldest sister said, "Come, see little Sootface. Her clothes are birch bark and weeds. Her moccasins are stiff and cracked. Yet she goes to find a husband!"

Next the middle sister shouted, "Look at little Sootface! Her hair is burned too short for braids. The smell of cook fires clings to her. Still she hopes to find a husband!"

Soon all the village was laughing at her. But the young woman continued on her way, never once looking back.

After a time Sootface met the hunter's sister, who was drawing water from the lake. She greeted Sootface kindly, and they began talking.

Suddenly, Sootface said, "There is a handsome man walking toward us. Do you know him?"

The hunter's sister said, "You can see him?"

"Yes, he is carrying a beautiful bow."

"Of what is his bow made?"

"A rainbow!"

"And how is it strung?"

"With white fire, like the Milky Way, the Path of Souls."

The hunter's sister embraced Sootface, crying, "You are going to be my brother's bride and my own sister!"

She led Sootface to the wigwam. There she poured water into a big pot and mixed in sweet-smelling herbs. Sootface found her hurt and sadness washed away as easily as the ashes from her face.

The hunter's sister gave her a dress of soft white buckskin decorated with beads and quillwork. Then she combed Sootface's hair with a magic comb that made it long and thick and shiny as a blackbird's wing. This she plaited into braids.

"You have made me beautiful," said Sootface when she looked at her reflection in the pot of water.

"Your beauty was merely hidden beneath the scars and ashes," said the other woman kindly. Then she called her brother into the lodge.

"What is your name?" the young man asked gently.

"Sootface," the girl said, blushing.

He smiled and shook his head. "Your eyes shine with such joy that I will call you Dawn-Light. Today I will carry a gift of game to your family as a sign of our betrothal."

Then his sister said, "Come, radiant Dawn-Light, and sit beside my brother. Claim the wife's place by the door flap. From now on this is your home."

At these words, Dawn-Light exclaimed:

Now, I am happy,
Now, I am certain,
That I have found my husband,
My new sister and new home.

They were married soon after. Everyone was
pleased, except Dawn-Light's two older sisters, who
had to do all the cooking and cleaning themselves now.